# To Dust

AMY LAURENS

# OTHER WORKS

### SANCTUARY SERIES

Where Shadows Rise
Through Roads Between
When Worlds Collide

### KADITEOS SERIES

How Not To Acquire A Castle
How Not To Ring The Hero's Bell
How Not To Take Over The World

### SHORT STORY COLLECTIONS

Of Sea Foam and Blood
Darkness and Good

### NON-FICTION

How To Write Dogs
How To Theme
How To Create Cultures
How To Create Life
How To Map (2019)

Find other works by the author at
www.amylaurens.com

# TO dust

INKLET #20

# AMY LAURENS

Inkprint PRESS

www.inkprintpress.com

Copyright © 2019 Amy Laurens
First published in *To Dust And Other Stories*,
Inkprint Press, 2013.

All rights reserved. No part of this book may be reproduced in any form or by any electronic or mechanical means, including information storage and retrieval systems, without permission in writing from the publisher, except by a reviewer, who may quote brief passages in a review.

This is a work of fiction. All characters, organisations and events are the author's creation, or are used fictitiously.

Print ISBN: 978-1-925825-19-0
eBook ISBN: 9781386091479

www.inkprintpress.com

*National Library of Australia Cataloguing-in-Publication Data*
Laurens, Amy 1985 –
To Dust
66 p.
ISBN: 978-1-925825-19-0
Inkprint Press, Canberra, Australia
1. Young Adult Fiction—Dystopian 2. Young Adult Fiction—Zombies 3. Young Adult Fiction—Short Stories

First Print Edition: October 2019
Cover design © Inkprint Press
Interior art © Amy Laurens

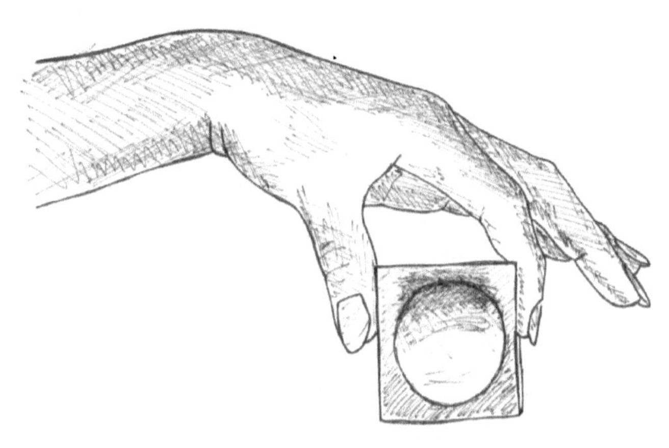

# TO DUST

Sometimes running away is the hardest thing you can do. What I want, what I really want, is to turn around right now and plunge back into the midst of the Maliche, let their rotting, stinking bodies surround me, and kill as many as I can before I die. For Mum. For Dad. For Joss.

God, please let Joss get away. Mum and Dad might be gone, but please, please... save him. I left him climbing for a rooftop, and the Maliche can't climb, and he might be safe enough— but I have to run, and running is so, so hard when all you want to do is die.

I can't die though, not today. Today

I have to live, because in my backpack, weighing me down like guilt, is the box. It's a perfect cube I can balance on one hand, sharp-edged and shined to perfection—a magic box, the only hope we have of stopping the Maliche forever. And I want to stop them more than anything else in the world, more than I want to die, because while there are Maliche, no one dies.

And so I run, heading north in a town that runs toward the battle in the south, running for life and death and salvation along a road whipped by the wind and smogged with dust.

From dust created, to dust returned. Only that's exactly it: with the Maliche on our doorstep, there is no return. I've seen the bodies they leave behind, twisted, gruesome things with flesh squeezed until the insides pop, left in the sun to ferment with a rictus of pain on their faces. And the eyes. The eyes are the worst.

No. Running away is hard, but it must be done. Humanity needs to die.

It is dusk three weeks later when I cross the stream to the Forest in the North, a forest fenced in by iron and water and dust. The Maliche are not our only enemies, though these others at least can be bargained with—and bargain I shall, for though legend states that the box I carry is the only thing powerful enough to save us from the Maliche, the box is magic, not Tech. Our only hope is to persuade the residents of the Forest in the North to help—and that is not a bargain easily broached.

I reach the iron fence that surrounds the forest, and iridescence plays over the latticework. If I lean in close I can nearly hear it hum. So much life. Too much.

Beyond the fence the aspens cluster densely, blocking out the sky, and under their shade it is already night. The shadows stretch and shift, not a mere absence of light, but something deeper, something more restless. I swallow and rub the sweat from my palms.

The wrought iron gate is cold. That I expected, but not the way the cold seems to reach for me, ice gripping my fingers and drawing me in. My tongue fixes to the roof of my mouth as I wonder whether the iron will let me go... But I push the gate open, and aside from a slight play of colour and the sheen of nervous sweat, my hands are unchanged.

I close the gate behind me without turning my back on the forest. Another fence pens me in, this one not of iron to keep the Wise Ones in, but of ivy and holly and tamper, built to keep the humans out. I wonder briefly how I will alert them to my presence—but footsteps sound on the path ahead of me, feet rustling in the thick carpet of dead leaves and organic matter. The Wise Ones have their magic, after all.

I press my hands to my thighs, willing them to steady. When the Wise One appears behind the next gate, I am thoroughly prepared, and yet not at all. My role as box-protector has allowed me many privileges; it isn't just pictures of the War I've seen.

And yet, no picture could do a Wise One justice. The eyes are so much more alive than any image can capture, and that sets my shivers running faster, because it makes me think of Maliche and corpses and clear, sea-green eyes staring brightly in festering corpses.

The Wise One's eyes glow too, though not a fevered burn so much as a glory—for the Wise One *is* glorious, even if its too-long fingers remind me of spiders and its hair is too silky and static to really be hair, and its skin glows with faint iridescence. Its features are fine and perfect, but the shoulders are broad, and I can't decide if it's male or female. When it speaks, even its voice provides no clues—a melodic timbre that could belong to either sex.

"Come." Its eyes linger for a moment on my backpack, then with-out further ceremony it turns and walks away.

I follow. As I pass through the gate a tingle washes over me, and I know I've entered the forest for real. A restlessness rises up in me and I want to run just for the sake of feeling wind-fingers in my hair and the burn of used muscles.

The Wise One turns off the path. I struggle to keep pace, feet tangling in vines and saplings and hidden hollows, ankles bashing against rocks and tree roots. I'm so much noisier than the Wise One, but it doesn't seem to mind.

The woods grow darker and I can't tell if it's because it's getting late or simply because the aspen canopy, interspersed with poison oaks, thickens overhead.

Probably, it's a matter of both.

Instinct tells me I have been walking for at least a half hour, following a silent beacon in woods too full of whispers and too empty of creatures to be real. I could be afraid, if I'd ever bothered to believe the rumours.

We stop, and the back of my neck prickles. Eyes green and blue and gold glow in the dimness before Wise Ones step forward, melting out of the shadows into reality—and in front of us, slightly above and closer in to the circle than all the rest, a Wise One who is unmistakeably female, hair sun-bleached and glorious, eyes brighter than brass, gown shimmering with the promise of deep blue skies and sun-drenched fields—a Summer remembered only in distant memory, before the sky became the pale, washed out expanse of now.

Without thinking, I dip down onto one knee, trembling with the knowledge that my quest is so nearly at its end.

"Arise, Imber of Lyons," the Queen of the Fae says, and I obey, because it never occurs to me to do otherwise. She smiles at me and butterflies burst in my stomach. "What is it you would ask?"

I struggle out of the straps of my backpack, lost for words, and, fumbling with the zipper, I manage to extract the box. I hold it out in front of me, heart pounding in my ears. "I bring a gift for the Queen," I say, because this is what must be said. My voice trembles only a little. "I... We need your help."

The Queen takes the box and her movement is an entire flock of gem-winged butterflies taking flight, flashing in imagined sunlight. She stares at it, and I bounce on my toes with nerves and anticipation. But then she frowns, and the box falls from her hands. She hisses as though she has been burned.

I quail. Her stare is a predator, devouring.

"You *dare* bring Tech into my forest?" she hisses, forked tongue flickering and eyes wider than the trees.

My palms hurt, and I realise it's because I'm on my knees in the dirt, sharp twigs and gravel cutting into my skin as I shelter the box with my body. "I'm sorry!" I sob as wind rises around us. "I didn't know!" The box is *Tech*?

"Enough!" The Queen raises her hands and wind springs up around us.

"This cannot be here!"

Magic encircles me. I am drowning.

Emotions dissipate as my mind breaks free from my body like a raindrop from an eave. I watch passively as the waves of hate and fear and sorrow swamp over me. The waves are beautiful, colours of summer tinged with the heat of fire, the iridescence of magic flashing like fish inside them.

I watch as it surrounds me, crashes over me, closes in. I take my last breath and the air smells like fire and soot, like sorrow and mourning, like over-ripe apples wasting in the last breath of autumn.

The waves crash against the box and it turns to ice. I gasp, shuddering, as the box absorbs the magic.

I am not dead.

I am not dead, but the box in my hands is ice and my limbs sear with heat, my eyes streaming, and the air is dry, so unbearably dry, but I am alive and the box is protecting me, absorbing the flow of magic, channelling it, and I can feel it building, and any moment now—

I gasp as the power explodes from the box, shooting up, up, up into the air.

The world stills. For a moment I stand there, gasping like I've forgotten how to use oxygen, and I think that I am saved.

Then the Queen speaks, and the terror in her voice stops me breathing altogether. "What have you done?"

At first I don't know what she means, but then my hands grow warm, and I stare in horror at the box, glowing ember-orange. I've seen something like this before, in a dream, or a memory... A box glowing, like mine, right before—

"Get down!" the Summer Queen screams, and this time I am grateful for my impulse to mindlessly obey.

I fling the box away as far as I can and duck, arms shielding my head. Something cool washes over me mere instants before the world explodes in white light and sound, and I'm pinned to the ground as sonic waves break and the world's foundations tremble.

It's some minutes before my vision clears and I can see what's happened. As far as I can see, there is nothing, nothing but char and ash, flat as pond water, untouched as glass.

"Was it not enough," the Queen asks, and I whirl to face her, "that you destroyed the forests of Lorien? Does it not matter that the fields of Elysium burned? Do you care not that the waters of Atlantis boiled and the mountains of Avalon crumbled? Did all this not satisfy the human need for destruction, that they must send you here, to destroy the last of our homes?"

My cheeks burn. "I'm sorry. I didn't know."

The Queen makes a dismissive gesture and turns her back on me.

Anger flushes through me. It isn't my fault that the box we thought was our salvation turned out to be a Trojan. I didn't mean to destroy her home by bringing it here.

But it might be a good tool to destroy the Maliche. "I didn't know," I say again, this time with more heat. "I was told the box was magic."

The Queen whips around to face me.

I shrink back from her fury.

"I would burn you to a crisp where you stood." Her voice is tight with control, but I hear what she means nonetheless. "But I do not wish to trigger another *event.*"

Her disdain is so strong I am nearly knocked over by it, but the sense of her words permeates through to my consciousness. "Trigger?" I say. "But the box is Tech, not magic."

The Queen's jaw works and I have the sense that she is wondering how much to tell me, how much I do not know—and wondering why I do not know it.

"I know nothing," I say, splaying my hands in a gesture of innocence. "Please." My voice is so quiet I can barely hear myself. "We still need your help."

She sniffs, but a moment later she has the box, holding it with the barest grip of her fingertips, lip curled in distaste. She stares at it for a moment before offering it to me. "It is Tech," she says, "but its power has died. Mine must have awoken it."

I fumble at the box as she hands it over and my fingers brush against hers. Sparks snap and fly. Dead power. She must mean its battery chip. Tech used to have those, before the War.

The knowledge of how to make them was lost and the cables that used to crackle with energy sagged dormant, then fell to decay many years past, but I have carried the box northwards for over a year; I have been shown things, I have been in Oseena's Library, and I have seen what they called 'electric'.

"But if it's electric," I say musingly, "how did your power activate it?"

The Queen shrugs. "Electric. Magic. They are all energy in some way."

I look at the box, then out at the horizon. It's completely flat, the southern mountains hidden behind the curve of the earth, with not a hill or a tree or a tussock to break the unending view.

I did that, I, with the box. Imagine what it might do to the Maliche.

Then I realise, and blink. "Did you save us?"

The Queen stares at me haughtily. "I used my magic to shield us," she says as though it were obvious. "I used energy to deflect energy."

"But why did you not save the whole forest? Could you do that?" I press.

Her shoulders droop. "Yes," she murmurs. "I could. If I was prepared."

"Oh." My stomach twists for her, but this still means my plan is possible. "Could… could you shield a town? If you were prepared?"

She shakes her head. "A… What is it you call them? A block? Perhaps. A few blocks. Not a town."

I chew my lower lip. A few blocks might be enough. "Come with me."

Her eyebrows lift.

"We can wreak vengeance together. I know the box ruined your home, but I'm only here because the Maliche are ruining mine. Come with me, help me end them, and then…" I hang my head. "Then you can punish me however you like." The word is punish, but we both know that really I mean kill, and I know without a doubt that she can do it—just as I know that death by her hands would be merciful compared to life at the hands of a Maliche.

The Queen's lips quirk. It isn't a smile, but it's something. She takes one last look around, drinking in the remainders of her home, then pierces me with her gaze. "I might just do that, Imber of Lyons."

I nod. We have a deal.

It is hardly a surprise when the Queen wraps me in her arms and soars away, airborne. For a heart-stopping moment I fear she will kill me—a long drop, sudden stop—but then it becomes clear that we are heading south, to Oseena, last remaining stronghold of humanity.

We land in the middle of the tarred main street and are surrounded by the cautious pause of people surveying us from behind the closed doors of multi-storey buildings, mostly steel and concrete and glass. My breath jags at the familiarity of the street; a long time ago, my home looked just like this.

Gradually, people filter out onto the footpaths, curiosity overwhelming their caution. The glittering beauty of the Queen beside me makes the street even more ragged, duller and more dismal than ever before, and I am conscious that she make me appear plain too, and that this is a town that has reason to be wary of strange creatures.

At the corner up ahead, people shift suddenly aside, and a man tears from them, running towards us.

I inhale sharply.

My chest is going to burst. I can't breathe. My eyes sting with tears and all of a sudden I've forgotten how to swallow, and it doesn't matter, none of it does, and it doesn't matter about strange creatures in Oseena or that I've destroyed the Wise Ones' home, and it doesn't even matter that I am an angel of death, bearing destruction in my palms, because here, *here*, where all hope was supposed to be lost, there is a man and his son running towards me, arms outstretched while wordless cries erupt from their throats and I know them, I know these men, and the taller one scoops me up and presses me to him and I cling to him harder than I've ever clung to anything before, and I burst.

"Daddy."

Joss clings to us both like he might die if he lets go, and my father runs his hands through my hair and squeezes me and his fingertips are like knives.

"Imber. Imber. You're alive."

"So are you." I hug them both tight and pray that we will stay that way.

It doesn't take long to convince the Council that the Queen is an asset and an ally. A quick demonstration of her power leaves them speechless, and my explanation of the box—its power, its reaction to the Queen's power—turns their eyes to saucers.

Still, the biggest shock comes half an hour into the discussion. While the Council members debate endlessly back and forth, the Queen is growing restless. Eventually she stands, and she is using her power in some way because immediately every eye is drawn to her spectacular form.

"Enough," she says. "You have debated this enough. You have seen my power; you have heard of the power of your precious box. What yet stands in your way?"

The Elderman eyes her thoughtfully before standing. "Your Majesty." He bows low. "I accept that you have power beyond our imaginations. I might even believe that you were willing to wield it for our benefit, though I've no idea what Imber has done to convince you."

I squirm under his gaze.

"But this box. We were told it was magic. You say it is Tech. We have Tech." He indicates the walls of the Council chamber, hung with relics of ages past: hand guns and rifles, automatic weapons and pistols. There is even a grenade or two. "None have harmed the Maliche in the slightest, for the Maliche are not creatures born of Tech. How do we know this box will be effective against their magic?"

The Queen, who merely glanced at the armoury covering the walls, leans forward. It's a tiny movement, but every person in the place is breathless, hanging on her whim. "Because," she said in a voice just above hearing, "this box was not the only. It was one of twenty."

The Council members' eyes mirror my own shock.

"Yes," she says. "*The* twenty."

> *And twenty shall destroy the earth;*
> *Unmake the world, reduce the worth*
> *Of all the evil taken hold.*
> *Twenty boxes death unfold.*

Not just a box; a Box.

There is no further discussion. We go to war.

We have chosen to fight from the rooftop of the Town Hall, the Queen and I. The people will gather below in the square, where the Queen can easily shield them. From here, it is only a block to the inner fence, easily visible over low rooftops. I survey the crowd that has gathered and my stomach twists to think that these represent the last of humanity.

A hand on my arm distracts me, and I turn. Dad. My throat closes.

"Please," he says, eyes so sad they are like bruises. "Does it have to be you?"

I stare out over the people, rolling the words around in my mouth. Does it have to be me? Really?

"Please, Imber. Let someone else go. Let *me* go."

I laugh, a withered, cracked sound. "You would have *me* be the survivor? No," I say, because my future is clear now, and I remember that the running is the hard part, that being the sole survivor in a family that fought to the death is the burden. I shake my head.

"That is your burden to bear, this time."

His jaw twitches as his shoulders deflate, and he hugs me tight enough to break a rib—but then he lets me go. I don't expect he'll ever hug me again.

And so we climb to the roof together, the Queen and I, as my father resumes his place in the crowd. My heart pounds with nerves and anticipation; there is so much that can go wrong, and so few ways for this to go right. We find our corner with a good view to the edge of town and both sets of fences, and I shiver. Now we wait.

A shout to the right draws my attention, and a few blocks down at the edge of town they are rolling back the gates, shifting the wagons—and a man runs through, red scarf blazing. The Maliche have been sighted, heading towards the town. My heart pounds. They're coming and here, now, at last, the running ends. I raise my hands, the smooth, soulless weapon perfectly balanced on one palm.

"It will need more power than last time," the Summer Queen says abruptly, shifting beside me. "You must direct everything I have."

I tremble. Her magic nearly swept me away last time; can I withstand a greater onslaught?

Footsteps, loud enough to shake the earth. Men's faces blanch, children weep, and women steel themselves for the onslaught. "They come." The whisper crackles through the crowd. "They come."

The Maliche pour across the dry, dusty landscape, shambling masses of rotten, putrid flesh, skin stripped away to reveal muscle and sinew and bone, and there are many, so, so many, and my courage quails.

There must be five times more than when I was here last; so many people consumed, bodies rotting while still alive, souls imprisoned forever inside a walking horror.

For them, I must channel the Queen's power. It is withstand her full strength, or withstand the Maliche.

And so I nod, and I know: the running is over. Today, it is my day to die.

I will never see my father again. Perhaps it is easier to run, after all.

The Queen offers her hand to me. "Ready?" she asks.

Down below, lining the main road as far as I can see, it is a sea of faces, more people than I could have believed—and few, so precious few to be all the survivors in the world. My eyes roam over the crowd, and I don't want to look for him, I don't want to see him, but—of course—he's looking back for me, and our eyes meet, and he nods, just once, the way quiet men do when they are proud.

"Yes," I say. "I'm ready."

I take the Queen's hand, and the power begins to flow.

A commotion; some of the Maliche have breached the outer fence and are running towards the inner.

My stomach twists. "Hurry," I murmur.

"I am," the Queen gasps, and she is breathless with the speed of the power flowing from her into me, and it knocks me over and sweeps me away, and I'm drowning in the wave again with magic flashing like iridescent fish until I remember the box, and it slams up like a wall of ice and blocks the power, absorbs it, channels it.

I can't hold it; it's too strong.

"Hold it!" the Queen barks.

I can't.

I can't, there's too much.

*"Hold it!"*

I hold, hold, and when I cannot hold it any longer, I burst like a sun going nova. I just have time to sense the

Queen throwing her shield around the crowd below, and then... nothing.

It's over. The box has won. Dimly, I know the Maliche are burning, limbs thrashing and flailing in the flames and I see them fall and the light in their eyes extinguish.

In minutes, the advancing army is nothing but glowing embers, the outer blocks of the city reduced to rubble and ash.

The people below us cheer.

I turn to the Queen. "Will you kill me now?"

"No," she says. She raises her arms limply. "I have used it all." Spent, she crumbles slowly to the ground, eyes closing before she vanishes in a puff of glittering dust that smells of summer—to dust, like the Maliche, like her home—like the people cheering in the street will now one day be.

I bow my head over the memory of the Queen and cry, because it hurts to

be the one left alive—and because I am
grateful to her for her gift, the final gift
of dust.

# THE MAKING OF
## *TO DUST*

This was a strange little story to write, not because of the contents, but because of the way I wrote it. Like *Cherry Blossom* (Inklet #16), it was partially a product of a Holly Lisle course I was working through at the time (I highly recommend her courses to anyone interested in writing).

This time, though, instead of an idea seed, I had a process that I wanted to try.

In addition, I had been teaching (high-school English) for a couple of years now, and for the first time ever through happy circumstance I had the opportunity to teach a semester-long creative writing course to a class of Year 12s.

Nothing, I thought, like a demonstration exercise in progress.

So I set out to write this story with virtually no idea what I was going to write, only the idea of this process: write until the story stuttered, go back and read what you've written so far and figure out what promises you've made to the reader. What threads have you included, what have you foreshadowed, what have you hinted might happen?

Fulfil those. Write again until you stutter, and go back and repeat the process.

Then, of course, I gave the first draft to my class as fodder for them to practice their critiquing skills on.

What is the heart of this story? I asked them. Where and how does it work for you? Where can you see the stuttering, and what would you personally do or recommend to fix it?

It was an illuminating experience, for all of us. And although I didn't write another story this way again that

I can recall, and although for many years after this I continued to basically outline most of my work, ironically enough I've now come full circle: the method I used to write this story is quite similar to a method called cycling that a lot of well-known writers use, and that I've been using for a couple of years now. *When Worlds Collide,* the third *Sanctuary* book, was written almost exactly like this, though I had to cycle back through books 1 and 2 as well to catch all the promises I'd made.

It's a fun—and freeing—way of writing, and it's funny coming back to this story and seeing in it the seeds of what would eventually become my main writing process.

It would be remiss of me not to finish by thanking the members of that Year 12 class (any remaining errors are, naturally, mine). Shannon, Bec, Becca, Lauren, Anna, Alice, Phoebe, Natasha, Laura, Shan, Vanessa, Sarah,

Tricia, Ellie, Miranda and Reeva: you guys were a fantastic class of amazing young people, and I hope that by now, you have truly found your voice in the world, whether that be through creative writing, or through some other avenue. Thanks.

# DOWNLOAD YOUR FREE EBOOK

When you buy a print book from Inkprint Press, we like to say THANK YOU by offering you the ebook for free!

Please head to
www.inkprintpress.com/inklets/20/
and the use the coupon 20INK to get your copy of this Inklet in epub AND mobi today!
(Coupon will only work once.)

# Read more by Amy Laurens!

# WHERE SHADOWS RISE

## CHAPTER ONE

THE DOORBELL RANG. That doesn't sound exciting in and of itself, but let me assure you: it was the most heart-pounding thing to happen all week. It was my birthday, I was home alone, and because of the stupid witness protection business, I'd been stuck in the house all summer. I hadn't even been allowed out to see friends, because we'd arrived in town at the end of last year with only three school weeks to go—so I didn't have any friends.

Well. I had friends, but they were back in Melbourne, and I wasn't allowed to contact them for fear someone would track down our new location. Lucky me.

Anyway, it was my birthday, I was alone because Mum and Dad had gone to do something regarding birthday surprises and Anna had inexplicably chosen to go with them, and the doorbell had just rung. I stared at the closed door, heart pounding, while our chocolate Labrador, Veve, tried to chew it down. Was I going to open it?

Of course I was going to open it. The chances of it being a mobster were slim to none; for starters, a mobster wouldn't have rung the bell.

I opened it.

"Miss Tanning?" The deliveryman raised a questioning eyebrow and cocked a digital pen at me.

I nodded, heart flip-flopping, and scrawled a fair impersonation of my signature on the digital pad.

He handed over a small, brown-paper parcel with a handwritten address, and departed.

I closed the door behind him, throat dry, and stared down at Veve. On the one hand, yay birthday present. On the other, holy crap, someone had our address. That was *not* a good thing.

It became even less of a good thing when I noticed that the parcel was indeed addressed to a Miss Tanning: a Miss *Anna* Tanning, as in my sister, not me, Emma Tanning.

Anger bubbled up in my chest, hot and tight, and the parcel protested in my grip.

Veve whined softly.

"How could she *do* this?" I whispered to Veve.

I turned the parcel over. It was from Kade, Anna's frogging ex-boyfriend. Who apparently wasn't an 'ex' after all.

Urgh. I ground my teeth. "You know what?" I asked Veve.

She looked up at me with her liquid brown eyes, tongue lolling as she smiled.

"Screw it. If Anna can get interstate mail from people who aren't even supposed to know we exist anymore, you and I can go for a walk on my birthday. What do you think?"

They say dogs don't speak English, but Veve sure as heck knew the word 'walk'—though I think in her vocabulary it was something closer to 'Magical Trip To Disneyland' and less like 'Comparatively Bland Meander Through Trees'.

She tucked her tail right under her butt and shot down the hall, whirling in frantic circles a few times at the end before pelting back as I retrieved her lead from the drawer in the front cabinet.

I rolled my eyes as I clipped her lead onto her collar. For my troubles, I got slimed right up the nostrils. "You're disgusting, you know that?" I wiped off the worst of the dog slobber on the shoulder of my shirt. She just grinned.

Out on the street, she leapt and twisted madly. "Hair-brain," I told her, snapping the lead to get her attention. "It's just a walk."

She just snorted—and stiffened. I followed her gaze to where a flock of corellas pecked their way through the dry grass at the end of the street.

"Veve!"

My shout was in vain: the lead burned through my fingers and Veve shot down the road, a chocolate bullet howling death and destruction for all things feathered.

I cursed her to the lower circles of doggie hell. Which probably involved, I don't know, a world devoid of birds, cats, people, sunshine, and walks, if Veve was anything to go by.

"Veve!" If the sight of the mad Lab-rat barrelling toward them hadn't scared the birds off, my shouts would have. "Come back here *now!*"

Predictably, she ignored me, pounding down the slope, through the fringe of gum trees, and down the narrow stairs between giant granite boulders that led to the river.

"Stupid frogging brainless beast of a stupid frogging dog," I muttered as I followed. "If Mum gets home before we do and freaks out, I swear, I'll pluck your tail hairs out."

Empty threats, obviously, but Mum's freak-out wouldn't be. Her thoughts would go straight to the day Anna nearly died—and I wouldn't blame her.

I should have left a note. Urgh.

The stairs ended and I found myself on a track broad enough for two twisting along a creek the colour of bitter tea. Tussock grass clustered in spikes—where the eucalypts would let it—and hot summer sunlight glinted from the leaves. Somewhere to my right, downstream and in the opposite direction to the house, Veve barked. I exhaled like a whale coming up for air and set out after her.

Veve bounded out from the under-growth in front of me, a dolphin leaping through water, tongue flapping with every bound. "Stupid mutt," I told her under my breath.

She didn't care what I thought (of course), and saved a leap for the last minute so she could plant muddy feet on my hips as I tried to catch her collar.

I straightened, about to insult her some more, and realised that she'd gone stiff again, ears pricked and mouth tight, listening down the path.

My neck prickled. Someone was coming. A second later, I heard footsteps in the gravel, and a low, male voice, humming, or maybe singing softly.

My chest constricted, and just as suddenly my hands were slick. Chances were it was just a stranger out for a midday stroll, but my stomach wound knots about my memories and

I smelled the hot concrete and melting asphalt, old oil and stale urine of the Lilydale train station where the body had been hidden in a toilet stall, the body of the girl who'd looked like Anna.

I had to get off the path.

"Come on, Veve," I said, pulling her close, white-knuckled as I stepped into the undergrowth. The tea tree scrub protested, but I shoved my way through anyway, glancing over my shoulder as the humming grew louder.

I kept going until I couldn't hear footsteps any more, until the wind swallowed the hum that sounded too like the warning cry of a hive—danger, we're working here, come close and get stung. I didn't want to get stung; visions of a blood-streaked face refused to be blinked away.

Only Veve tugging brought me back to myself, and I realised firstly that I was holding the lead way too tight, cutting off Veve's air supply, secondly that the reason my cheeks were suddenly cold was because I'd been crying, and thirdly that I'd found the creek again, looping back parallel maybe fifty meters or so from the path.

Abruptly, I dropped Veve's lead and strode forward to kneel by the water. I dipped my hands in. A shiver slid through me at its chill, and I scooped it up to wash my face.

Flinging the excess water away, I gulped at the air, deep, calming breaths all the way down into my belly, and visualised a river washing away the blood from my thoughts, just like the police psych had taught me.

Once the space behind my eyes was calm and black, I drew in one last forceful breath, and opened my eyes. Perched on a rock by the creek, I hugged my knees to my chest as cool water lapped at my toes. Veve was a little upstream, just before the creek bent back toward the path, doggy paddling in circles in a deep spot where the water broadened to maybe ten meters across. In front of me it was broad but shallow, only ankle deep, its path torn to white foam by the rocks.

And—I gasped. In the middle of the stream, glittering in the sun like a piece of fallen sky, was the hugest butterfly I'd ever seen.

Which was pretty huge; besides the fact that I grew up visiting the Melbourne Zoo with its impressive butterfly house every Christmas since I could remember, Mum and Dad had taken us up to Brisbane for a family holiday two years ago, and we'd seen giant tropical butterflies bigger than my hand.

This one, bright blue with black edging like a Ulysses, was bigger than both my hands put together.

And then it turned around.

Okay. I'd grown up reading fairy tales as much as the next person, and although I'd had a horse-crazy stage instead of a fairy-crazy stage like Anna had, I'd seen all her paraphernalia.

Still, none of it prepared me for finding something that looked exactly like a fairy, standing smack in the middle of a creek in boring, back-water Nowra.

I'm pretty sure my eyes were only hanging in their sockets by a thread.

And then it talked.

Her face lit up like a cloud had just uncovered the sun as she spotted me. "Hi there!" she said, fluttering over.

I just stared, heart pounding against my ribcage as though it wanted to run away from the absurdity of it all. "No," I said. "I'm hallucinating."

The fairy frowned. "I don't think so."

I shook my head. "No. No, things like this do not happen. Things like this aren't *real*." I stood, backing up a step.

The fairy sighed. "I promise. I'm quite real."

"You would say that, wouldn't you," I said, eyeing her. "Veve!" I waved at the dog and hopped from one foot to the other, trying to lure her in with the promise of play. "We're going now!"

Veve, adorable beast that she was, landed a little upstream and shook vigorously before trotting toward me. I backed hurriedly away from the bank, dancing to keep Veve's attention.

"Wait!" the fairy cried, wings snapping out and propelling her a couple of feet into the air. "You're a Traveller! I need to talk to you!"

"Uh huh, sure," I said as I wound the lead around my hand and set off back into the bushes. This was punishment for leaving the house, obviously. The universe was out to get me, reminding me forcefully that once you started disregarding some rules, who knew what other rules you'd end up flouting.

The rules of physics, for example.

I glanced back once, right before the bushes hid the stream altogether. Blue flashed, high up, but I ducked to get a better view and it was only the sky. I scowled. Stupid fairy. Stupid universe. Served me right for leaving the house in the first place. Urgh. "Come on, Veve," I said, snapping the lead. "Even if the house is prison, at least it's *sane*."

I was stomping so furiously as I burst out onto the path that when a figure rose from a stoop only a couple of steps away, I squeaked in surprise.

I scowled. People rarely surprised me; usually I could tell without trying that someone was near. I really must have been off in my own little world.

I glowered at the boy who lived to make my school life a misery. "What are you doing here?" I snapped. "Isn't it bad enough that I have to deal with you on school days? Which, by the way, don't start until tomorrow. You're ruining my holidays."

Okay, so maybe that was a little harsh, but come on. It was *Scott*. I'd arrived in town with three weeks left in the school year, and he'd spent every day of them humiliating me in front of his mates, and I didn't care for a repeat this year.

Scott eyed me warily, which was a strange expression on him.

Usually he strode around like he knew without a doubt that he was too good for the world, and also—somewhere deeper, somewhere I'd only caught a glimpse of once or twice— that it had nothing left to throw at him that could hurt.

Occasionally, in my more generous moments, I wondered what had happened to make him look that way.

Mostly, however, I just wondered why he was such a moron.

"What are you doing here?" he asked, voice dripping with accusation and suspicion.

My hands fisted of their own accord, and beside me Veve's hackles rose as she chimed in with a low-pitched, rumbling growl. I flicked the free end of the lead at her nose. "Nothing," I said, in a rousing blaze of wit. "What are you doing?"

He scowled. "You shouldn't be here."

For one heart-stopping instant I thought he meant out here generally, walking around, as if he knew what had happened and why I'd hidden away all summer. Then I realised he was nodding into the undergrowth. I rolled my eyes. "I might be a city slicker," I bit off, "but I'm not stupid. I made enough noise to scare off a herd of elephants, let alone any snakes that might have been lying around." The thought chilled me, though; I *hadn't* been thinking about snakes when I'd hurried off the path. One badly-timed footstep and a brown snake bite later, and I could be a dead body too.

But Scott had moved on, stalking off down the path. He had nice shoulders, I'd give him that much. Pity he couldn't derive his personality from them, instead of whatever dead weight it was he kept inside his head for brains.

Beside me, Veve growled again, louder this time, more urgent. I snapped the lead at her and stared after Scott's retreating form, trying to think of something cutting.

It was only when Veve growled for the third time that I realised she wasn't even facing Scott. Instead, she was looking back into the bushes—and something dark was flickering in there, deep in the shadows of the trees.

My chest squeezed in on itself and adrenalin shot through my body. Veve's growling grew louder until it broke in a bark, something midway between slavering and terrified, and I realised my tongue was stuck to the roof of my mouth. Carefully I peeled it away, unable to tear my eyes from the shifting darkness in the bushes. There was no discernible form, just shadow, darker than it should have been this soon after midday, and a pervasive sense of dread clamping down on me like an on-coming storm.

Veve began backing away, hackles prickling, growl rising and falling like thunder. I glanced down at her, back to the shadows—and they were closer, much closer than they had been.

I turned and bolted.

Keep reading! Head to
http://www.amylaurens.com/book
s/sanctuary/where-shadows-rise/
to buy your copy now!

# ABOUT THE AUTHOR

AMY LAURENS is an Australian author of fantasy fiction for all ages who lives with her husband and two children.

In addition to the *Sanctuary* series of portal fantasy stories set in Nowra, Australia, Amy has written the humorous fantasy series *Kaditeos: Mercury*, beginning with *How Not To Acquire A Castle*, as well as a whole bunch of non-fiction for writers and non-writers alike.

You can find out more about Amy at her website, www.amylaurens.com.

# INKLETS

Collect them all! Released on the 1st and 15th of each month.

INKLET #007
SEVENTY
LIANA BROOKS

INKLET #008
A Final Request
for Mercy
AMY LAURENS

INKLET #009
the kitten psychologist
vs.
the kitten's owners
THEA VAN DIEPEN

INKLET #010
Answer the
Question
AMY LAURENS

INKLET #011
Happily, Red
AMY LAURENS

INKLET #012
the kitten psychologist
tries to be patient
through email
THEA VAN DIEPEN

INKLET #013
DRAGON
Tuesday
AMY LAURENS

INKLET #014
RED PLANET
REFUGEES
LIANA BROOKS

INKLET #015
the kitten psychologist &
What The Kitten Did
THEA VAN DIEPEN

INKLET #016
Cherry Blossom
AMY LAURENS

INKLET #017
Alone
AMY LAURENS

INKLET #018
the kitten psychologist & The Kitten Come To A Conclusion
THEA VAN DIEPEN

INKLET #019
LEVEL NINE
LIANA BROOKS

INKLET #020
To Dust
AMY LAURENS

INKLET #021
Interchange
AMY LAURENS

INKLET #022
Emalia's Lanterns
LIANA BROOKS

INKLET #023
Dear Santa
AMY LAURENS

INKLET #024
The Quilt-Maker's Scrap
AMY L. LAURENS

www.ingramcontent.com/pod-product-compliance
Lightning Source LLC
Chambersburg PA
CBHW031035190726
48286CB00003BA/1187